# CALViN COCONUT

## TROUBLE MAGNET

### Graham Salisbury

illustrated by
Jacqueline Rogers

WENDY
LAMB
BOOKS

Published by Wendy Lamb Books
an imprint of Random House Children's Books
a division of Random House, Inc.
New York

This is a work of fiction. Names, characters, places, and incidents either are the
product of the author's imagination or are used fictitiously. Any resemblance to
actual persons, living or dead, events, or locales is entirely coincidental.

Visit us on the Web! www.randomhouse.com/kids

Educators and librarians, for a variety of teaching tools, visit us at
www.randomhouse.com/teachers

*Library of Congress Cataloging-in-Publication Data*
Salisbury, Graham.
Calvin Coconut in trouble magnet / Graham Salisbury ;
[illustrations by Jacqueline Rogers]. —1st ed.
p. cm.
Summary: Nine-year-old Calvin catches the attention of the school bully on the day
before he starts fourth grade, while at home, the unfriendly, fifteen-year-old
daughter of his mother's best friend has taken over his room.
ISBN 978-0-385-73701-2 (hc) – ISBN 978-0-385-90639-5 (glb) –
ISBN 978-0-375-89393-3 (e-book)  [1. Family life–Hawaii–Fiction.
2. Schools–Fiction. 3. Bullies–Fiction. 4. Kailua (Oahu, Hawaii)–Fiction.]
I. Rogers, Jacqueline, ill. II. Title.
PZ7.S15225Cal 2009
[Fic]–dc22
2008001415

The text of this book is set in 13.5-point Baskerville BE Regular.

Book design by Angela Carlino

Printed in the United States of America

10 9 8 7 6 5 4 3 2

First Edition

Calvin Coconut is for
Annie Rose

I am so lucky to be your dad
—G.S.


For Sage and Amaya

—J.R.

# Prob'ly an Idiot

Maybe you know the feeling of how junk it is when summer ends. The good times are over. You start thinking about school, homework. Getting up early again.

And there's *nothing* you can do about it.

But I say, forget that. Get out there and squeeze the last drop of fun out of summer.

Which is why I was down at the beach with my friends Julio Reyes and Maya Medeiros. We were watching a kiteboarder zip over the ocean. I couldn't believe how fast he was going. "Ho, man, look at that guy go!"

Julio whistled. "Like a rocket."

The hot sun sparkled on the blue-green bay. The kiteboarder topped a small wave and let his kite pull him high into the sky. He did a flip and came back down. Perfect.

"Holy moley," I whispered.

All three of us lived a couple blocks from the beach on the same dead-end street, in a town called Kailua, on the Hawaiian island of Oahu. Across from our small one-story houses, patches of jungle blocked our neighborhood from a fancy golf course. High above the jungle, green mountains sat under hats of white clouds.

Julio elbowed me. "That guy's a famous kiteboarder."

"No joke? What's his name?"

Julio pinched his chin. "I forget. Something."

2

Maya laughed. She was cool, and really good at sports. Better than me and Julio. She had a skateboard and a brown belt in tae kwon do. She was born somewhere in China. The Medeiros family adopted her.

We were sitting on a sandy rise under a stand of ironwood trees just above the beach. It was a breezy Thursday morning, and we pretty much had the place to ourselves.

The kiteboarder swung around and raced toward shore. When he got as close as he could before hitting sand, he slowed and sank to his knees. His kite settled down onto the water like a small parachute. He stepped out of his wakeboard and pulled his kite in, then spread it out on the sand.

"Hey," he said. "You kids mind watching my gear? I need to run over to the pavilion."

"Sure!" I sprang to my feet.

"Thanks. Be right back."

The guy dropped his wakeboard, harness, and control bar and headed up over the rise.

The wakeboard was black with red stripes.

It had foot grips and looked new. Nice. I glanced over my shoulder to see if the guy was coming back. Nope. I waggled my eyebrows at Julio and Maya. "Watch this."

I stepped into the foot straps. "Bring on the wind!"

"You better get off that, Calvin," Maya said.

I picked up the control bar, which was attached by cables to the kite spread out on the beach. "Yee-hah!" I gave the cables a flip. The kite caught a puff of wind, rose a foot, and settled back down. Ho, man, this was so cool!

I grinned at Maya and Julio.

Just then a strong gust whooshed down the

beach and caught the kite. The kite blossomed and snapped up off the sand.

"Calvin!" Maya pointed.

I was still grinning at them when the wind grabbed the kite and whoomped it out like a sail. It shot down the beach, ripping the control bar right out of my hands.

"Grab it!" Julio shouted.

I leaped off the wakeboard and stumbled after it, Maya yelling, "Get it! Get it! It's flying away!"

The control bar bounced along the sand, just out of reach. It skipped out over the water, came back over the sand, and skipped

out again. I dove for it and landed on my belly. But I managed to grab the bar and hang on.

The wind was strong! I couldn't slow the escaping kite. It dragged me over the shallow water on my stomach. It fishtailed me up onto the sand, then back into the water again.

"Calvin!" Maya shouted, racing down the beach with Julio.

I bounced and banged over the water, swallowing salty gulps of ocean.

"Calvin! Let go!" Julio called. "You'll drown!"

But I would never let go.

A quarter mile down the beach the wind finally let up. The kite sank onto the sand. I sank into the water, gripping the control bar with white knuckles.

Julio grabbed the kite. Maya waded into the waves. "You all right?"

I staggered up, coughing.

Maya grinned when she saw that I was okay. Just soaked, bruised, scratched, and covered with sand. "You look like you fell into a cement mixer."

"Uh-oh." Julio nodded toward the pavilion.

The kiteboard guy was racing toward us, shouting, "Hey! What's going on?"

He ran up, breathing hard.

"The wind grabbed your kite, mister." I handed him the control bar. "We, uh . . . we saved it."

The guy looked at me, then at Julio with the kite bunched and overflowing in his arms. "I must have been careless. Hey, thanks for running it down for me."

"Yeah, no problem."

He laughed. "No problem? You look like roadkill."

He gathered up his equipment and started back up the beach.

"Hey!" I called.

The guy stopped and turned back.

"Are you a famous kiteboarder?"

"*Pshh*. I wish."

I frowned at Julio. "You idiot."

Julio shrugged.

Maya pointed at my arms and chest. "Yikes! Blood."

I looked down. Cuts and scratches ran across me like spiderwebs. "Cool."

Maya stared at me. "I think *you* might be the idiot, Calvin."

"And I think you're prob'ly right." I grinned.

Julio slapped my back. "You sure know how to end summer with a bang, bro."

# 2

# Like a Sister

I rinsed off at the beach park pavilion. Sand was caked in my hair, my ears, my underwear, and the pockets of my shorts. I squeezed the water out of my T-shirt and threw it over my shoulder.

"Hey, Cal," Maya said. "Are you supposed to meet your mom here?"

"No," I said, checking the scratches on my arms and chest. They stung, but not too bad.

"Well, look." Maya pointed with her chin.

Just down the way, Mom and my six-year-old sister, Darci, were spreading a blanket out on the grass. Weird, I thought. Mom hardly ever comes to the beach. She's always working.

We headed over. Mom saw us and waved.

"What are you doing here?" I asked.

Mom gasped when she saw my cuts and scratches. "Cal! What happened?"

"He went kiteboarding," Julio said.

Mom gaped.

"He just went in the ocean, Mrs. Coconut," Maya said.

Mom looked at me and sighed. "Well, anyway, I was hoping to find you here, Cal. I have something special to tell you and Darci."

"What is it?"

Mom glanced at Maya and Julio. "It's kind of a surprise."

I winced. Mom's surprises could be good. Or not.

Julio sat, always ready for a good surprise.

Maya knew better. "Let's go, Julio. I think this is private."

"Oh . . . sure." Julio sprang up. They left.

I sat down next to Darci. "What's up, Darce?"

She shrugged.

Mom smiled. A big smile. A big *fake* smile. Uh-oh.

She clapped her hands together. "Guess what, kids? Someone is coming to live with us, someone you're going to love. Isn't that great? Her name is Stella. She's fifteen."

I blinked. What?

Darci brightened. "You mean I'll have a sister?"

"Yes, Darci, she'll be just like a big sister.

Stella's mom and I were best friends in high school."

Sand must have found its way into my brain, because it wasn't working. Did someone say *big sister*?

"She's coming from Texas," Mom added.

"But why?" Darci asked. "Doesn't she have a house?"

"Of course she has a house, sweetie. Her mom just . . . well, her mom thinks she needs to get away for a while."

"Why?"

"Well," Mom said, then stopped to think. "Sometimes teenage girls and their moms need a break from each other. It will be good for Stella to live here."

"Big sister?" I finally said.

Mom snapped on that fake smile again. "It's so exciting, Cal. She's arriving Saturday."

My thoughts swirled like water going down a drain.

"I know it's kind of sudden," Mom added.

*Kind* of?. Then I thought, Hmmm. Maybe

this could be a good thing. "Are you going to make her the man of the house instead of me?"

Mom laughed.

I'd been man of the house since my now-famous dad, Little Johnny Coconut, hit it big with a song called "A Little Bit of La-la-la-love" and left the islands for the bright lights of Las Vegas. He never came back. That was four years ago. I was five.

Being man of the house meant responsibility. I wasn't so good with that.

"No," Mom said. "You'll still be the man of the house."

"A girl can't be the *man*," Darci said.

I frowned. Too bad. The man of the house had to do too much stuff. And do it right, too. Mom was always saying, "Why can't you pay attention? Be more responsible, Calvin, for heaven's sake?"

She was right. I was a goof-up. Sometimes a big one. I couldn't help it. Trouble zoomed up to me like a paper clip to a magnet. Look what had just happened with the guy's kite.

Or take yesterday, when Mom got all over me because I forgot to drag the garbage can out to the street. Now we had to wait a whole week for the next pickup. By then the garage will smell like dead fish.

I grumbled, "What's *man of the house* mean, anyway?"

"I know," Darci said. "It means you can grow a mustache."

"For real?" A mustache would be cool.

Mom chuckled. "That's something you don't have to worry about just yet, Cal."

Dang. "Do you think she'll laugh at our name, Mom?"

"She already knows."

"That's good."

*Coconut* was my dad's idea. He made it up. For a famous singer, *Little Johnny Coconut* sounded way more interesting than Little Johnny *Novio,* which was our real last name. Dad was so pleased with himself, he made the name legal. Now we were all Coconuts.

Mom leaned back and let the sun warm her face. "This is going to be a terrific year, kids. Stella's coming to live with us; Macy's is moving me up in the jewelry department; Darci, you'll be a *first* grader; and Calvin, wow—you're going into fourth grade."

I stroked my upper lip. Should I grow a pencil mustache? Or one of those walrus ones?

"Will Stella go to school?" Darci asked.

"Tenth grade," Mom said. "She'll babysit, too."

My mustache dream popped. *"Babysit?"*

Mom patted my knee. Another bad sign. "Let's

give her a big welcome when she gets here, okay?"

Darci clapped and nodded.

Mom looked me in the eye . . . with that fake smile . . . and with her hand still on my knee.

"What?"

"There's one more thing. Um . . . honey . . . we're going to give Stella your room and move you out to the storage room in the garage."

"What!"

"A teenage girl needs her privacy."

"But Mom, the storage room is full of bugs!"

"Ledward will help you clean it out."

"But . . ."

My thoughts tumbled like wild surf. I didn't mind bugs that much, but sleep in the storage room? That was crazy.

Mom shook my knee and winked. "I want you to fix the lock on your bedroom door so Stella doesn't get stuck in there like you always do. Then you can start cleaning out the storage room."

My head felt like a firecracker had just gone off in there. "Mom, can I go live at Julio's house?"

"You're going to love Stella, Cal. You'll see."

# Centipede

Back home, I put dry clothes on and went out to look at the storage room. I inched open the door. I poked my head in. Dark. Dusty.

You gotta be kidding. Prob'ly I should just run away from home. It smelled like damp cardboard.

Boxes of junk cluttered the floor, and spiderwebs connected everything like Halloween decorations. When I turned on the light, six roaches raced for cover and a monster centipede slithered past my bare foot.

"Yahh!" This one was as long as a rat's tail!

It stopped. I could tell it was glaring at me, like it was saying, You want trouble? Come on, I'll give you trouble. Those things could sting like a wasp. But for some reason I liked centipedes. All those creepy legs.

I spotted an old peanut butter jar and grabbed it.

"Hey," I whispered to the centipede. "Don't attack, okay?" I got down on one knee. Carefully, I scooped the centipede into the jar and capped it. "Gotcha!"

It squirmed in the jar. I held it up. "Don't worry, I won't kill you." I could never do that. But Mom could. "If we're going to be roommates I sure don't want you running loose."

I nearly leaped out of my skin when

someone tapped my shoulder. "Jeese, Julio!
You scared me."

"What you doing in here?"

"You wouldn't believe it if I told you."

"Try me."

"Later."

"Maya has money. We're going to the
store."

"What for?"

"Just come."

"I gotta tell my mom where I'm going. Here, hold this."

Julio staggered back. "No way!"

"He can't bite you. He's in the jar."

"I don't care if he's on the moon, I'm not touching it."

I put the jar on top of the garbage can. "Don't open it. He's not very happy right now."

I forgot all about the centipede long before I followed Julio and Maya through the gate in Julio's backyard. I forgot to fix the lock on my bedroom door, too. But I could do it later.

Maya jingled the change in her pocket. "Found it in the couch."

We headed over to Kalapawai Market to buy some sodas and say goodbye to summer vacation. The next day was Meet Your Teacher Day.

Julio kicked a paper cup someone had run over. "I hate when vacation ends."

"Yeah, but what you gonna do?"

We headed toward the small park across the street from Kalapawai Market.

"Can you believe it?" Maya said. "Tomorrow we'll all be in Mr. Purdy's class!"

Julio whooped.

I jumped and punched the sky, because everyone who'd ever been in Mr. Purdy's fourth-grade class said he was the best teacher on the planet. Especially the boys, because Mr. Purdy still thought he was in the army.

"Bring on the homework," I said. "Not!"

Julio scowled and shoved me. "Aw, man, why'd you say that? Now you ruined it."

"No, I never."

"Yes, you did, you had to go and remind me of—"

"Hey," Maya said, grabbing Julio's arm. "Look."

A cop car with its lights flashing skidded to a stop in front of Kalapawai

Market. A huge policeman stepped out. He hitched up his pants, grabbed a notebook, and went into the store. The lights kept flashing.

"Ho, man!" Julio said. "They got robbed!"

# 4

# Sinbad

Whenever I see a cop car with flashing lights I almost stop breathing. "Maybe he'll bring a prisoner out in handcuffs."

"Shhh," Julio said. "Watch."

A few minutes later the cop came out of the store . . . with someone we knew.

"Ho," I whispered. "It's Tito."

"He finally got caught," Julio said.

Tito Andrade was a sixth grader at our school, Kailua Elementary. For years he'd been vacuuming stuff out of our pockets—pennies, nickels, dimes, candy, beef jerky, dried squid.

Tito robbed me once. He did it with a smile and said, "Thanks for the donation, Cocodork." I didn't complain, and for sure I didn't tell the principal. If I had, Tito would've made me pay. And not with money.

Tito's head was bowed. Long dark hair hung into his eyes.

"He doesn't look too happy," Julio said.

As the cop put Tito in the backseat of his car, a lady from the store came out to talk.

"Do they take sixth graders to jail?" I asked.

"No," Julio said. "They take them to probation."

"Where's that?"

"It's like a bad-boys' home."

The cop and the lady talked by the cop car.

All I could see of Tito was his head in the back window.

Finally, the lady waved her hand, saying, No big deal.

The cop looked at Tito in the car.

"He's going to let him go," Julio said. "Watch."

Julio was right. The cop opened the back door and helped Tito out. Tito blinked and looked around.

"He fell asleep," Maya said.

Julio humphed. "Prob'ly seen that backseat a hundred times."

"Yeah," I said. "Like his second home."

"You know what's his middle name?" Julio said. "Sinbad."

"How you know that?"

"I saw his health form in the school office— Tito Sinbad Andrade."

"Perfect. He sins, and he sins bad," Maya said.

We cracked up.

Tito turned and looked across the street.

When he saw us laughing, his eyes narrowed.

We stopped laughing. Quick. That wasn't smart, I thought.

Tito was still looking at us as the cop put his hand on Tito's shoulder. They talked for a while. Tito nodded, and I imagined him lying, saying, I'll be good, Officer, don't worry, I won't steal nothing, I'm honest.

He must have been a good talker, because the cop finally got back into his car, turned off the flashing lights, and drove away . . . without Tito.

Tito watched the police car head down the road.

Then, slowly, he turned and looked across the street.

"Uh-oh," Julio said.

Tito swaggered over and stood looking down on us. "Whatchoo insects was laughing at?"

I acted surprised. "Us? We weren't laughing."

27

"No lie, I heard you."

I scratched my head like I was confused, buying time. Think, think. "Uh, uh, the cop was funny, Tito, not you."

Tito eyed me. How come I was the one to speak up? I should have let Julio do it. I searched for more.

"Uh . . . uh, the cop had . . . uh . . . he had a hole in his pants . . . in the butt."

"Why you tell me that? You think I'm stupit?"

"No, Tito. For real. It was a big hole, and you could see his underpants."

Julio snorted.

"Yeah?" Tito said. "Okay, what color was his underpants, ah? Tell me that."

"Uh . . . blue."

Tito's eyes narrowed to slits.

Maya stared at Tito, unafraid. Tito ignored her.

Julio jumped in to change the subject. "What did the cop want, Tito?"

Tito shrugged. "They thought I took something."

"Did you?"

Tito grabbed Julio's shirt. "You accusing me?"

"No—no, Tito, I never." Julio threw up his hands in surrender.

I stepped in. "They got it wrong . . . right?"

Tito let go of Julio and got down into my face. "I know you was laughing at me, Cocodork. You lucky I'm in a good mood right now, because if I wasn't, I would mess you up." He spat on the grass. "You see me in school tomorrow, stay out of my way."

"Sure, Tito, no problem."

He walked away, glaring over his shoulder.

I should have kept my mouth shut.

Julio fell back, spread-eagle on the grass. "Ho, man, we almost got killed!"

"He doesn't scare me," Maya said.

I cringed. Now Tito was going to watch us like a shark. We'd just put ourselves on his radar.

# 5

# Excited

*Be-beep. Be-beep. Be-beep.*

I groaned when my alarm went off at six-thirty the next morning.

I covered my head with my pillow.

It was Friday. Meet Your Teacher Day.

Real school started on Monday.

*Be-beep. Be-beep.*

"All right, all right."

The clock was on the windowsill, leaning against the screen. I had bunk beds and slept on the top, so I had to reach down to slap it off.

I got up and pulled on my jeans, then dug around for my special Little Johnny Coconut T-shirt. Might as well start fourth grade right.

I grabbed my new backpack and headed for the door.

It wouldn't open. Dang. Locked in again. I got my pocketknife and jimmied it into the thumb lock.

The lock popped open. "Yes!"

Darci was standing on a stool in the bathroom trying to brush her hair. I squeezed in next to her and found my toothbrush. "How come Mom's not doing that for you?"

"She said I had to learn how to brush it myself."

I did my teeth and tossed the toothbrush back into the drawer. Darci's brush got tangled in her hair and she couldn't get it out.

"Want some help?"

Darci dropped her hands. The brush stayed in her hair.

I worked the brush out slowly and handed it back to her. "Put water on it first. I saw Mom do that."

Darci stuck it under the tap and tried again. It worked.

"There you go."

I went into the kitchen.

"Congratulations!" Mom said. "You passed the alarm clock test. It's a big day, Cal."

"Yeah, sure." I said it like it didn't matter. I couldn't sound all excited, like some small kid. I grabbed the orange juice out of the fridge and guzzled it right from the carton.

"Calvin!" Mom snapped.

"Sorry." I put the juice back.

"Listen," Mom said. "I'll drop you and Darci off on my way to work, but you have

33

to walk her home after school. I'll be back around six." Mom worked at Macy's in the Ala Moana Shopping Center on the other side of the island.

"I want you to keep an eye on her until I get home. Can I count on you, Calvin?"

"Sure, Mom." The walk home was only a mile or so.

"When Stella gets here, she'll watch Darci after school. But today she's your responsibility."

"I can do it."

"Just don't forget. . . . Oh, and Ledward's coming over this afternoon to help you clean out the storage room."

I scowled, remembering. I had to move in with the roaches, spiders, lizards, ants, earwigs, mice, centipedes, and wet-cardboard stink. "Mom, why can't Stella and Darci share a—"

"No, Cal."

I sighed. "Fine."

"Please walk Darci to her class this

morning, too. Just for today, so she knows where to go."

"Sure."

Mom smiled. "Thank you, Calvin. I need your help."

"I know, Mom."

She brushed my cheek with the back of her fingers. "You're excited about fourth grade, aren't you?"

"Yeah, Mom. That's me . . . excited."

# Raising Dust

On my way out to the car, I remembered the centipede. The jar was still on the garbage can. The centipede didn't look so good. Maybe it needed air. Or food. What did those things eat, anyway?

I quickly stuffed the jar into my backpack. If Mom saw me with a centipede, she'd make me squish it.

"Darci's teacher's name is Ms. Wing," Mom said when she dropped us off at Kailua Elementary. "I called her last night and told her you would be bringing Darci to class, since I can't."

"I know what to do, Mom."

"That's my boy!"

We waved as she drove off. "Let's do it, Darce."

Ms. Wing was standing at the door to Darci's new class-room. She was Chinese, like Maya. Her super-shiny black hair flowed all the way down her back. Wow, I thought. She looks like she just stepped out of one of Mom's magazines.

Darci looked up at her.

"Uh . . . this is Darci," I said. "She's in your class."

Ms. Wing leaned over with her hands on her knees. "Good morning, Darci. I'm Ms. Wing, and I'm so happy to have you in my class."

Darci opened and closed her mouth, like a fish.

I nudged her with my elbow.

"Hi," Darci squeaked.

"I'm her brother."

Ms. Wing stood and reached out to shake hands. "Nice to meet you, Darci's brother."

We shook. Ms. Wing looked at the list of student names taped to the door. "Let's see . . . Darci, Darci. Oh, *you* are Little Johnny Coconut's daughter."

Darci beamed. "He's a singer."

Ms. Wing sang, "'A little bit of la-la-la-love' . . . that was a *very* popular song!"

"I gotta go," I said, before she sang more.

"Thank you for bringing Darci to class, Darci's brother."

"No problem."

On the way to Mr. Purdy's room, I ran into Julio and three of his four younger brothers–Marcus, Diego, and Carlos. "Scat!" Julio told them. "Find your classrooms." They ran off. "If my mom has one more kid I'm moving into our fort."

"I have to move into my garage."

"That junky storage room?"

"Uh-huh . . . some girl is coming to live with us."

"What girl?"

I shrugged. "Hey, look at this place."

Kids were everywhere, running and shouting and raising dust all over the playground.

"Like a party," Julio said.

"You think Mr. Purdy will let us sit together?"

"We can ask."

"Yeah, let's." I studied the dusty playground. "You see Sinbad?"

"*Shhh*. Don't call him that. What if you say it to his face?"

"No way."

Julio tapped my arm. "There's Rubin and Maya. Hey! Over here!"

I hadn't seen Rubin Tomioka in two months. He didn't live on our street, and anyway, his parents sent him to Japan in the summer to live with his grandparents and learn Japanese. Rubin was always in a good mood.

I lifted my chin as he and Maya walked up. "Hey. Check this out."

I pulled the peanut butter jar out of my backpack and raised it to my eyes. The centipede was curled around the bottom.

Julio stepped back. "Why'd you bring *that*?"

"I like it."

"Holy cow!" Rubin said. "He's big! Where'd you get it?"

"I caught it in my . . . my new bedroom."

Maya shuddered. "I'd move out. That's too creepy."

The bell rang. I stuffed the jar away.

Maya looked worried. "What if it gets loose in your backpack?"

"No," Julio said. "What if it gets loose in *class*?"

# 7

# Boot Camp

Mr. Purdy had arms so strong they looked like they could crush rocks. His thick neck grew out of a bright green silk shirt that hung out over khaki pants. His black hair was buzzed, army style.

Mr. Purdy smiled as we walked up. "Mr. Coconut, Mr. Reyes, Mr. Tomioka, and our skateboard wizard, Miss Medeiros. You all finally made it to fourth grade."

"Hi, Mr. Purdy," we said.

Rubin bounced on his toes. He just couldn't stand still.

"You know my classroom isn't the playground, right?" Mr. Purdy asked.

"Yes, Mr. Purdy," we said.

"Whew!" Mr. Purdy pretended to wipe his brow with relief. "I'm sure glad to hear that, because when I saw your names on my class list, I thought I might have to install a cage in the back of the room, just for you knuckleheads—but not you, Maya."

We grinned. We knew Mr. Purdy from out on the playground. Last year at recess he was always yelling, "Hey! You boys are playing too rough! Cool your jets! You hear me? This isn't a combat zone."

But Mr. Purdy never stayed mad. Sometimes he would pull up his sleeve and let us look at the tattoo on his arm. U.S. ARMY was written in a banner under a scowling eagle.

Julio nudged me.

"Oh yeah, uh, Mr. Purdy, can me and Julio sit together?" I asked, fingers crossed.

Mr. Purdy leaned close and whispered, "Not on your life."

"Huh?"

"I've already assigned seats," Mr. Purdy said, straightening back up. "Your names are on your desks. But if you two can go a week without getting into trouble, maybe I'll reconsider your request."

Good enough. We could do that.

Julio gave me a thumbs-up.

We went in.

Hoo, that room was yappy as a mynah bird tree. I covered my ears.

Fourth grade!

I saw Doreen, Ace, Kai, Levi, Emmy, and Reba. They were in my room last year. And Shayla, wearing a pink dress.

I winced and ducked behind Julio. For some reason, Shayla liked me. Last year she wouldn't leave me alone. Julio called her

Shayla the Snoop because she was so nosy. I crossed my fingers that maybe there was a mile between her desk and mine.

Julio nudged me. "Look."

A new kid was standing off by himself. He looked like he might barf any minute.

"He just moved in next door to me," Maya said. "He kinda . . . stands out."

"No kidding."

The new kid was blond, a haole, a white boy. Everyone else in Mr. Purdy's class had black or brown hair. In fact, in the whole

school there were only about ten kids with blond hair.

"What's his name?" I asked.

Maya shrugged. "All I know is he's from California."

Cool. California.

"Hey." I pulled the jar out of my backpack.

"Anybody know what these things eat?"

"Ants," Maya said.

Julio shook his head. "No. People. Keep that lid on tight."

I loosened the lid.

"Don't!" Julio jumped back. "You want it to escape?"

"It needs air. Look, it's dying."

"It's faking. Just look at it through the glass."

Mr. Purdy clapped his hands. I put the centipede away. "All right," Mr. Purdy said. "Take your seats."

We scrambled to find our desks.

I got lucky. Mine was up front by the window, and next to Ace, who was a good guy. Shayla was on the other side of Ace. Way too close.

"Hey," I said to Ace.

"Hey."

I looked to see where Julio and Rubin were.

Ho! Mr. Purdy had placed us three in opposite corners of the room, as far away from each other as possible. The fourth corner went to the new kid.

"Welcome to fourth grade!" Mr. Purdy said. "Or, as I like to say, welcome to boot camp, where at the end of the year, you will be all that you can be. Are you ready?"

"Boot camp! Boot camp!" we all chanted.

I looked at Julio way in the back.

He pumped his fist.

*"Sssssss,"* Mr. Purdy hissed through his teeth.

Everyone stopped joking and turned to look at Mr. Purdy. Awesome, I thought. He hisses like a snake.

"When you hear that sound, what does it mean?"

Rubin bounced up and waved. "It means shut your yaps!"

The class roared. "Bingo," Mr. Purdy said. "Looks like you got a little smarter since I saw you last, Mr. Tamioka."

Rubin turned red. He sat down and fiddled with something on his desk.

I fiddled with something, too.

It needs air. It's dying.

Just a little crack of air.

# 8

# Escape!

The centipede was lying on its back with its hundred feet in the air.

Maybe Julio was right, and it would jump out.

But it looked dead. I'd killed it.

I glanced up when Mr. Purdy said, "If you haven't met him yet, this is Willy. His family just moved to Kailua from . . . was it Los Angeles, Willy?"

Everyone looked at Willy.

"Pasadena," he mumbled without looking up.

"Right," Mr. Purdy said. "Pasadena is in Los Angeles County, which is in Southern California. Has anyone here been to California?"

No one raised a hand. I sure hadn't, though Dad had said to come visit the mainland sometime. Rubin had been to Japan, but that was it. Some kids in that classroom probably hadn't even been on a car ride to Honolulu.

I leaned forward and peeked down the front row. The new kid was staring at his desktop.

"Good to have you in our class, Willy," Mr. Purdy said.

Willy nodded.

I turned back to the centipede. Slowly, I unscrewed the lid all the way and looked down into the jar.

The centipede sprang to its feet, slithered up the inside of the jar and out onto my wrist.

Yah!

I froze, gaping as it snaked over my hand and dropped into my lap.

"Mr. Coconut," Mr. Purdy said. "Is something going on over there that's more interesting than I am?"

I looked up, my mouth half open.

"Calvin?"

I looked down. The centipede scurried over my shorts, down my leg to my foot, and onto the floor. It zipped under the desk behind me, heading through a forest of wiggly legs. And only I knew it.

"Mr. Coconut!" Mr. Purdy snapped.

I was too stunned to answer.

Mr. Purdy shook his head. "Ace, will you please change seats with Shayla." It was a command, not a question.

Ace got up and moved.

Shayla plopped her books on the desk next to me.

"Hi, Calvin," she said. "Did you have a nice summer?"

"Uhnn."

Mr. Purdy was brutal.

He turned back to the class. "Now might be a good time to bring up the subject of responsibility. Your whole fourth-grade experience will be based on it. Who can tell me what *responsibility* means?"

Hands went up. But not mine.

"Mr. Coconut, what does *responsibility* mean?"

"Uh . . . it means . . . take out the garbage?"

The class exploded in laughter.

Even Mr. Purdy smiled. "That was one of

my responsibilities when I was a kid, too," he said. "Still is."

I tried to smile, too, but I was going crazy thinking about that centipede. Was it smart enough not to crawl over somebody's foot and start a riot?

Mr. Purdy went on. "By *responsibility* I mean I'm going to hold you *responsible* for doing your best in this class. Respect me, respect each other, and respect yourselves. Give me the best you have in you, and I'll give you the best I have in me. Is it a deal?"

"Deal!" everyone shouted.

I plastered Mom's fake smile on my face and tried to look like I knew what was going on. But in my mind I was down on the floor looking under all those desks.

Where.

Was.

It?

# 9

# Pencil Race

I had three brand-new pencils in my backpack. I took them out, lined them up on my desk, and glanced back at Mr. Purdy, who was handing out papers to take home.

With my finger, I nudged the pencils toward the edge of the desk.

Closer, closer.

The pencils clattered onto the floor.

Mr. Purdy turned.

"Oops. My pencils."

Mr. Purdy turned back, shaking his head.

I got down on my hands and knees to pick them up. Too easy. They were right by my feet. I needed more time down there. I flicked them farther away.

Here, peedy, peedy, peedy, I said in my brain, like mental telepathy. Where are you? I winced when I saw something stuck to Shayla's shoe. But it was just muddy grass.

*Here, peedy, pe—*

There!

Not squished. It was moving along the wall, back by Rubin's desk. *"Pssst."* I tried to get Rubin's attention, but he was gazing out the window, picking his nose.

"Rubin," I whispered.

I pushed my pencils back toward the centipede.

"Calvin."

I looked up. Mr. Purdy was standing

over me. "Is this some kind of a pencil race?"

I shot up and banged my head on Kai's desk. "Oww."

"What are you doing, Calvin?" Kai said.

Everyone laughed.

"Back to your seat," Mr. Purdy said. "Now!"

I grabbed my pencils and took one last glance at the centipede.

Gone!

Mr. Purdy headed to the front of the room, holding up two fingers. "Two things," he said. "Rules. And lunch."

Rubin took his finger out of his nose. "Lunch?"

Mr. Purdy pointed toward the list of class rules on the wall near his desk. "Did anyone happen to read this?"

The rules were written in big black letters on yellow poster board.

# MR. PURDY'S FOURTH-GRADE BOOT CAMP RULES

1. Work hard and do the best you can.

2. Have fun learning new things.

3. If you don't understand something, ask for help.

4. If you want to speak, raise your hand.

5. Be kind and respectful to others.

6. Never laugh at someone else's mistake.

7. When the bell rings, remain in your seat until you are excused.

8. Say something nice to someone every day.

9. Drink lots of water.

10. Don't pick your nose.

Everyone laughed and turned to look at Rubin when they got to number ten. "I'm serious about that last one," Mr. Purdy said. "I don't want to find dried-up boogies under your desks."

Rubin turned bright red.

The class roared.

"Okay," Mr. Purdy said, rubbing his hands together. "I have a surprise for you today. In celebration of your first day in fourth-grade boot camp I'm treating you all to . . . lunch!"

A cheer erupted. Everyone but me stomped on the floor. "Lunch! Lunch! Lunch!"

I almost yelled, STOP! You might stomp on my centipede!

"Woo-woo!" everyone shouted.

Even the new kid joined in.

"Settle down," Mr. Purdy said, holding up his hand. "After long negotiations with Mrs. Leonard—that's your principal—I was granted permission to invite a good friend of mine over to cook for you. Uncle Scoop!"

"Woo-oo-oo!"

Uncle Scoop's Lucky Lunch truck was parked at the beach every weekend. Uncle Scoop served hamburgers, hot dogs, chicken and beef teriyaki, kalua pig and cabbage, tripe stew, malasada doughnuts, sweet juices, and big fat shave ice to cool us in the sun's burning heat. He sold all kinds of snacks, too: sweet whole plum, cracked seed, beef jerky, cuttlefish, dried squid, kimchee, and Maui chips.

I was starving just thinking of it.

"How do you know Uncle Scoop, Mr. Purdy?" Julio asked.

"Scoop and I grew up here in Kailua. After high school we went into the army together."

"Tell us about the army, Mr. Purdy."

The lunch bell rang.

"Looks like that'll have to wait, Julio. But we have all year. Right now it's time to eat." Mr. Purdy gave Julio a full-on U.S. Army salute. "Line up!"

I headed to the door, hunched over, looking one last time, thinking, Peedy, peedy.

Nothing.

But it was there.

Somewhere.

# 10

# SmackDown

While everyone else at Kailua Elementary headed over to the cafeteria, we swaggered like lottery winners out to the parking lot and Uncle Scoop's Lucky Lunch. "Rock and roll!" Rubin shouted.

"Hey, you!" somebody called from the crowd by the cafeteria. "Coco-dork!"

I stopped to look back.

"You!" Tito yelled again. "Coco-roach!"

Julio bumped into me from behind. "Pretend you can't hear him."

Too late.

Tito Sinbad Andrade came slouching over with some other sixth grader. Another new kid, but not haole, like Willy.

My friends stood with me. The rest of Mr. Purdy's class continued on to Uncle Scoop's truck.

"We meet again," Tito said, smiling. He tapped his chest. "You like my new shirt?"

It was a brand-new white World Wrestling Entertainment T-shirt. It said SMACKDOWN across the front. "Yeah, that's cool, Tito."

"My uncle got me um." Tito hooked his thumb over his shoulder. "Frankie Diamond wants to meet you."

Frankie was as tall as Tito and had a silver chain around his neck. He had straight white teeth and green eyes. His thick hair was spiced with something that smelled like oranges.

He crossed his arms and looked down on me.

Tito snickered. "Frankie thinks Little Johnny Coconut's songs are stupit."

"So?" I said.

Frankie Diamond grinned. "Good answer," he said. "You got guts."

*"Pshh,"* Tito spat. "What we doing with stupit fourth graders."

They slouched away.

"You're the stupid ones!" Maya shouted.

Frankie Diamond turned, surprised.

Maya made a fist and held it up. Frankie threw back his head and laughed.

# 11

# Uncle Scoop's Lucky Lunch

Everyone lined up at the lunch truck. Uncle Scoop beamed down from behind the counter in a white apron and yellow ball cap that said CAVEMAN KITESURFING on the front.

Mr. Purdy reached up to shake his hand, then turned and opened his arms. "Meet my new fourth-grade boot campers."

"Boot campers?" Uncle Scoop said. "Then you folks must be hungry!"

"Yeah!" everyone said.

"Step right up!"

The line burst ahead, everyone pushing and shoving.

"Come inside the truck," Uncle Scoop said to Mr. Purdy. "Help me feed this crowd."

Everyone cheered when Mr. Purdy showed his face behind the counter. "Have what you want," he said. "But choose wisely. I don't want your parents lecturing me on Monday."

"Yes, sir, Mr. Purdy, sir!"

Julio ordered teri beef with rice and macaroni salad. Maya got two Spam musubi, which was Spam wrapped in sticky rice and seaweed. Rubin went for a plate of rice and spicy hot pickled cabbage called kimchee.

I got one cone sushi and a bag of dried cuttlefish. Yum, so chewy and salty.

Willy, the new kid, frowned at the long menu.

Julio nudged me and whispered, "He doesn't know what all this food is."

"For real?"

Willy ended up with a hot dog and Maui potato chips.

"Hey, new kid," I said. "You want to try some of this?" I held up the bag of cuttlefish. For sure he'd like that.

"What is it?"

"Cuttlefish. Try some. It's good."

"What's cuttlefish?"

"Dried squid. It's chewy, like beef jerky."

Julio and Rubin crowded around us, Rubin working on his plate of stinky kimchee. I winced. "Back off with that stuff."

Rubin grinned, his mouth stuffed with food.

I held the bag of cuttlefish out to Willy. He reached in and took some out. He looked at it, smelled it. "Fishy."

"Yeah, smells good, ah? What's your last name?"

"Wolf."

"Wolf! Ho! Cool."

Julio nodded. "Yeah, that's a good name. Willy Wolf."

Willy stuck the cuttlefish into his mouth and started to chew. His look went from curious to anxious. He chewed some more.

I studied his face. "Good, yeah?"

Willy gulped the last little bit down. "Uh . . ."

"Try some kimchee," Rubin said, holding up his plate. It smelled like sulfur. I laughed, thinking Willy wouldn't get near it.

But he actually tried it. Impressive. I couldn't stand the stuff.

Willy let it sit in his mouth. He made a lemon face, then grabbed his throat. "Ack!" He coughed and spat it out.

Rubin leaped back.

Kimchee splattered all over our feet. Willy danced around, wiping his tongue off with his T-shirt. "Hot! Hot!"

Rubin roared, laughing his head off.

Willy spat. "What *is* that stuff?"

"Pickled cabbage and chili peppers." Rubin stuffed some in his mouth. "Yum."

"You got it all over my feet," Julio said.

He got it all over mine, too. "It's your fault, Rubin. You gave it to him."

"Yeah, Rubin!"

Rubin kept laughing, the doof. Julio flipped a fork of macaroni salad at him. He missed, and it landed in Doreen's hair. "Hey!"

Rubin thought that was hilarious, too. He tossed kimchee at Julio. It hit him in the face.

And the war was on.

In seconds the whole class joined in, food flying everywhere. "Food fight!" somebody yelled.

Something gooey hit me in the face. "Aw, man!"

"*Stop!*" Mr. Purdy shouted from the lunch truck. "Stop it! Now!" No one even heard him. Mr. Purdy stormed out and got right in the middle of it. "What are you *doing*!"

One by one we came to our senses, picking food out of our hair, brushing it off our clothes.

"Sorry, Mr. Purdy."

"We didn't mean to."

"We won't do it again, sorry."

"Sorry doesn't cut it!" Mr. Purdy said, his face angry red. "You are my *guests* here. Mr. Scoop came all the way to this school because I told him my class was exceptional. Well, I was sure wrong about that!"

We all fell silent. No one could look at him.

"Who started this?"

No one peeped, but I was thinking, Ask idiot Rubin.

"I asked you a question," Mr. Purdy said, his eyes on fire.

The new kid stepped forward. "I guess I did, sir."

Mr. Purdy studied Willy. Then he looked at

me, Julio, and Rubin, all of us speckled with pieces of food. "You four go get cleaned up. We're going to talk about this later."

We slunk away.

"Move it!" Mr. Purdy shouted.

We couldn't run unless we were on the playground, so we started fast-walking. I sped ahead, eager to escape Mr. Purdy's angry look.

At the cafeteria, I zoomed around the corner and smacked right into something. "Ooof!" It felt like I'd run into a cow. Stars winked, my head spun.

It was Tito Sinbad Andrade. He staggered back.

He was holding a small box of grape juice and must have squeezed it when we hit. Purple juice was splattered all over his brand-new *SmackDown* T-shirt.

"Oh, man," Julio whispered. "You are so dead."

# 12

## Haw!

But Tito didn't notice his shirt yet. *"Hey!"* he spat. "Watch where you're going!"

I felt a small lump rising on my forehead.

Tito looked at the grape juice dripping off his hand.

And all over his—

"Haw!" He stepped back, looking down at

his ruined T-shirt. His eyes bulged like golf balls. "My shirt!"

"Sorry, I didn't mean–"

Tito threw the juice box at my feet, stomped on it, and shoved me. *Wham!* "Look what you did!"

He raised his fist. I ducked, but before he swung, Mr. Tanaka came out of the library.

Tito held back, his fist shaking. He glared at me. "I get you after school," he whispered through clenched teeth. "You going pay for this!" He shoved me again, but not too hard, because Mr. Tanaka was watching. "You ain't seen the last of this, no."

Tito glanced at Mr. Tanaka and waved, as if saying, Hey, everything's cool, heh-heh.

Mr. Tanaka kept looking.

Tito banged past, bumping me with his shoulder, trying to brush away the ugly purple stains.

I groaned. In a single second I'd turned Tito's new T-shirt into his mom's next dust rag.

"It was an accident," I said to no one.

Willy stood gawking, watching Tito walk away. "Who is that guy?"

"Sinbad," Julio said.

"His name is Sinbad?"

"No, it's Tito," Julio said. "Sinbad is his middle name and don't ever call him that. Stay away from him . . . if you can."

I closed my eyes, thinking, I won't even make it home. Tito will pick his teeth with my bones!

We cleaned up in the boys' bathroom and headed back to the parking lot. Uncle Scoop's truck was still there, but no kids.

"Shoot. They went back to class."

We started back to Mr. Purdy's room.

"Is Coconut *really* your last name?" Willy asked. "Or was Mr. Purdy joking?"

"It's real now. My dad made it up."

"Why?" Willy asked.

But I wasn't listening. I was thinking: Right now Tito and that Frankie guy are probably deciding where they're going to jump me.

"Calvin?" Willy said.

"Huh?"

"Your name," Julio said. "Tell Willy."

"Oh. Yeah. Sorry. See, my dad's a singer, and he changed his name. It used to be Novio. Italian."

"You don't look Italian."

"My dad's Italian. My mom is Filipino, Hawaiian, and Chinese."

"Cool," Willy said.

"Hey, look," Julio said. "There's Uncle Scoop. We should, you know, apologize or something."

He was right. We messed up bad. "Yeah, let's do it."

So we went over and apologized.

But Uncle Scoop wasn't nearly as angry as Mr. Purdy. "Thank you, boys. I appreciate your apology." He shook his head and smiled. "I was in a few food fights myself, as a kid. And if you can keep a secret, so was your teacher."

Mr. Purdy!

I still felt bad. We'd goofed up. "We won't do it again, Uncle Scoop."

Unbelievably, he gave each of us two coupons for a free shave ice. "That's for apologizing. Recognizing and admitting you're wrong takes courage. Come see me down at the beach and have a shave ice. You know where to find me."

Rubin's face lit up. "Ho! Thanks, Uncle Scoop."

Uncle Scoop tapped Rubin's shoulder and winked.

"Wow," Willy said as we headed back to class. "Uncle Scoop is a nice guy."

"For sure."

"But . . . what's a shave ice? Is it like snow cones?"

We stopped and looked at Willy like, What?

"A snow cone is crunched-up ice with flavory syrup on it."

I said, "Right. Shave ice!"

Crazy, I thought. Willy never heard of that, or cuttlefish, or kimchee. He sure has a lot to learn. "Let me tell you about cracked seed," I said. "And don't worry, it's not hot."

"Does it stink?"

I laughed and slapped his back. He was okay, this haole kid. All he needed was a little education.

And all I needed was a giant bodyguard.

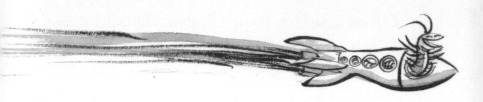

# 13

## The Rocket

Back in class, I sat gazing out the window. Mr. Purdy had written a topic on the board and I was thinking.

"Give me at least five complete sentences," Mr. Purdy said. "And remember to punctuate."

I reread the topic. *How I can be all that I can be.*

I liked that U.S. Army slogan. But all I could think of to write were a few words.

Like, *Study.*

*Try hard.*

*Don't pick my nose.*

I grinned. Mr. Purdy was funny.

*"Eeeeeee!"* somebody shrieked.

I jumped and whipped around. Doreen was climbing up on her chair, screeching like a hyena.

*"Eeeeeee! Eeeeeee!"*

Mr. Purdy hurried back to her.

"A *centipede*!" Doreen cried. "It crawled over my *foot*! *Eeeeeee!*"

"Calm down, calm down," Mr. Purdy said. "It can't get you up there. Where did it go?"

"I don't know! Get it!"

Rubin dove under his desk, looking for the centipede.

Maya pulled her feet up.

Julio stood by the door, ready to run.

Two girls sat on top of their desks, laughing.

I grabbed my hair and pulled. This can't be happening!

Everyone except Doreen was having a party. How cool was this? A centipede in class!

Mr. Purdy got down on his knees. "Anybody see it?"

I dove under my desk, calling the centipede in my mind: Here, peedy! Where are you, peedy, peedy?

"There it is!" Maya shouted. "It's running for the door!"

Mr. Purdy leaped up.

I banged my head on Kai's desk again.

Everyone was shrieking with delight, except Doreen, who was shrieking

with tears. I grabbed the jar out of my backpack and sprinted after the speedy peedy. Ho, man! This one was a rocket!

"Get it!" Doreen screeched. "Kill it!"

Mr. Purdy blocked the door. The centipede ran toward him. Mr. Purdy raised his foot.

"*Don't,* Mr. Purdy! Don't kill it!"

Mr. Purdy looked at me. He looked at the empty jar. "I see," he said, slowly lowering his foot. The centipede stopped and stood its ground. "You want to catch it for us, Calvin?"

I crawled up to the centipede and clamped the jar down over it. Trapped. It slithered up inside the glass. I flipped the jar right-side up and slammed the lid down.

I slumped back on the floor, catching my breath.

The whole class whooped and cheered and clapped.

Mr. Purdy stood looking down on me. He reached out and waggled his fingers.

I handed him the jar.

Mr. Purdy inspected the centipede. He

held it up for Doreen to see. "Got him. No need to stay up there on your chair."

Doreen didn't budge.

Julio crept back to his seat.

I looked up at Mr. Purdy.

"You," he said. "Come with me."

I stood and brushed myself off.

"Oooo," the class taunted as I followed Mr. Purdy to his desk.

*"Sssssss,"* Mr. Purdy hissed.

*"Sssssss,"* the class hissed back, then fell silent.

"All right," Mr. Purdy said. "The rest of you can go back to writing your paragraphs."

At his desk, Mr. Purdy admired the centipede, turning the jar in his hand. "Sure is a big one." He put the jar on his desk. With a screwdriver, he punched three holes in the lid. "Give the poor guy some air. He's had a hard day."

Not as hard as me, I thought. "What do they eat, Mr. Purdy?"

"Bugs. However, he can go for days without eating. But let's talk about you."

"Me?"

"What am I going to do with you? It's only the first day, Calvin."

I shrugged and looked at the centipede. It seemed to be saying, This is all your fault, Coco-fool. Get me out of here.

Mr. Purdy tapped his fingers on his desk. "How many times have you messed up today?"

I shrugged.

Mr. Purdy sighed. "Do I have to send you to the principal's office?"

"No, sir."

Silence.

"Tell you what. Next time, that's where you'll go. For now, I have something else for you. All this month, you're going to be our classroom greeter."

No, no, Mr. Purdy, I pleaded in my head. Not classroom greeter, please, no, because classroom greeters had to stand at the door and shake hands with everyone and say "Welcome to class," even the girls.

But I kept my mouth shut. It was better than going to the principal's office, where sometimes they called your mom.

"Go back to your seat, Calvin. See if you can write one simple paragraph without burning down the school."

"Yes, Mr. Purdy."

I slumped down in my chair and picked up my yellow pencil. I smelled the eraser, then stuck the pencil between my teeth and looked out the window.

When Tito popped back into my head, I bit down and snapped the pencil in half. I spat out slivers of wood and yellow paint.

How will I make it home alive?

# 14

## way Too Close

At the end of the day, everyone grabbed their stuff and lined up at the door. Except me. I stayed at my desk. Trapped. Like the centipede.

"Is something wrong, Calvin?" Mr. Purdy asked.

"No, sir." I dragged myself up and got in line.

"See you on Monday!" Mr. Purdy said.

The class burst out like ants from an ant hole.

I crept up to the door and peeked out.

No giant bodyguard, but Julio was there, waiting for me.

"You see Tito?"

"No."

"Quick," I said. "I got to get out of sight."

Rubin was waiting for us by the chain-link fence behind the school. On the other side of the fence was a grassy field. I had to cross it. Then I had to make it past the intermediate school, where Tito had a lot of scary friends. After that, there were long, bushy, hiding-place streets all the way to our neighborhood.

We started across the field.

Julio grabbed my arm. "Hey! You forgot your centipede!"

"Forget it. We can give it a name and make it the class pet."

"Fang," Rubin said.

I shook my head. "Not Fang, Stanley."

"Stanley," Julio said. "Why Stanley?"

"I like Stanley. Manly Stanley."

"That's cool, too," Rubin agreed.

My scalp started to tingle. Something didn't feel right. "We got to watch for Tito."

Rubin swerved over and bumped me. "Man, you sure messed up his shirt."

"Thanks for reminding me."

We made it to the intermediate school with no problems. There were lots of kids around, getting rides or walking home. Some were unlocking their bikes from the chain-link fence.

No Tito.

So far, so good.

Just past the intermediate school, Rubin waved and headed down his street. "Stay alive, bro."

Thanks a lot. I started to sweat. Tito could be hiding in any hedge or any bush in any yard, waiting to jump out.

The street ahead was quiet.

It looked safe . . . it felt safe . . . until Julio gasped.

I froze. "What?"

He pointed. Tito and Frankie Diamond were crouching in the shade of somebody's monkeypod tree. Tito hadn't spotted us yet.

But Frankie had. He nudged Tito.

Tito sprang to his feet.

I gulped. "Back! Now!"

Tito sprinted toward us, Frankie Diamond right behind.

I yelped and raced toward the intermediate school, Julio burning rubber beside me. We sped past the main entrance to the back parking lot. Nothing

to hide behind. No cars. No buses. No bushes. No nothing!

Except . . .

It was our only hope.

We leaped toward the huge garbage bins and scrambled up over the rim of the first one we came to. It was empty. But slippery black gunk grew on the bottom.

Julio pulled his shirt up over his mouth and nose. "Yuck!"

I clapped my hand over his mouth. "Shhh!"

I pulled my shirt up, too, because the smell was worse than some dog's terrible breath. But it was better than getting beat up.

I heard Tito shout, "Where'd they go?"

"Inside the school! Try that door!"

Feet thumped past on the blacktop. A door opened and slammed shut.

I inched up and peeked over the top. "Quick! Before they come back out!"

We struggled up and fell out of the garbage bin . . . and ran.

And ran.

And ran.

Close to home, we staggered to a walk, gasping for air. My hands were shaking. My legs felt like rubber. "That was . . . way . . . too . . . close."

Julio bent over, catching his breath. "Almost . . . home."

The word *home* hit me like a hammer. "*Darci!* I was supposed to walk her home!"

I turned and raced back toward the school.

"Wait!" Julio shouted. "They'll get you!"

I kept running.

# 15

## KING KONG

Amazingly, I made it to Ms. Wing's room without running into Tito and Frankie Diamond. The door was locked.

I banged on it. "Darci! Are you in there?"

My voice fell back into the empty schoolyard. "Dar-*ceeee!*"

Mr. Moto, the janitor, poked his head out of a classroom. "What you want?"

"My sister, Mr. Moto. Darci Coconut. Have you seen her?"

"Everybody gone. Go home. Nobody here."

Maybe she went home by herself, I thought. She could do it. She wasn't scared.

I took off.

Take the long way home. It's safer.

But why hadn't I run into Darci when I ran back to school to look for her? If she'd been walking home, I would have passed her.

Now I was really worried. I picked up my pace, jogging, then sprinting as thoughts of creeps and bad guys flooded my brain.

By the time I reached my driveway, I was sweating like a boiling crab and twice as mad. At myself. What kind of brother forgets his own sister?

I ran into the garage.

"Darci!"

I threw open the door.

She was in the kitchen, pouring herself a bowl of Rice Krispies. She looked up. "Hi, Calvin," she said, as if it was just any old regular day.

I slumped back against the door and sagged with relief. "I was . . . supposed . . . to walk . . . home with you. . . . I forgot."

Rice Krispies tumbled into the bowl. "That's all right."

All right? I slid down to the floor. I put my elbows on my knees and covered my face with my hands.

"When you didn't come, I just started walking," Darci said.

I shook my head. "Mom's going to kill me!"

"Why?"

I looked up. "Are you gonna . . . you know, tell her?

"Tell her what?"

"That I forgot to walk you home."

Darci cocked her head as if that thought hadn't even crossed her mind. "Should I?"

"Prob'ly, yeah . . . but . . . will you?"

Darci shrugged and took a bite of cereal.

"You can if you want to," I said. "I won't get mad."

Just then I heard an engine out in the driveway. "Someone's here." I sprang up and ran to look out the window, thinking maybe Tito got one of his high school friends to give him a ride. But it wasn't Tito.

"It's King Kong."

King Kong was Ledward, Mom's boyfriend. I don't know why I called him that, except that he was a hundred feet tall. His real name was Ledward Young. He was half Hawaiian and half a bunch of other stuff.

"He's here to fix up your new room," Darci said.

I groaned, remembering that disaster. Time to move in with the bugs.

Ledward parked his old army jeep on the

grass. It didn't have a top, like a convertible. He unfolded himself as he got out, wearing shorts, a Hawaiian shirt, and rubber slippers, like everyone else.

"Hey, boss," he said when I got outside.

"Hey."

Standing next to Ledward, I felt like a mouse. He told me one time, when *he* was in fourth grade he was as tall as his teacher. But the most amazing thing I'd learned about him was that he'd gone to school with Mr. Purdy and Uncle Scoop. They were all friends then, and were still friends now.

"Daniel treat you all right today?" Ledward asked.

"Who?"

"Mr. Purdy is what you'd call him, I guess."

"Yeah, he's cool. He calls our class boot camp."

Ledward laughed. "That would be him."

"He has a tattoo."

"He's a good man. The best."

I nodded, remembering the food fight and

the centipede, and how Mr. Purdy hadn't even chewed me out or sent me to the princi- pal's office for any of it. Except there was that classroom greeter job. I frowned. I'd have to shake Shayla's hand and say "Welcome to class, Shayla." Every day.

"Grab the toolbox off the backseat," Ledward said. "Let's go look at that storage room."

"Is Mom really making me move out there?"

"You don't want to?"

"Would you?"

"Sure. It would be like having my own place. Look at the view you got . . . mountains, river, the street. Better than what you have now, ah? Unless you like looking at the backyard."

He was right. All I could see from my old room was Darci's rusty swing set. Maybe the storage room would be okay after all. If we could get rid of the bugs.

Ledward's toolbox weighed about fifty pounds. But it smelled good, like oil. I set it on our garbage can. The hinged lid was puffed up now. The trash was starting to overflow. But it didn't stink too bad. Yet.

Ledward winked. "You ready?"

"No."

Ledward opened the door and flipped on the light. "Find a broom, boy. We got work to do."

# 16

# Stella

Just after noon the next day, Julio, Maya, Willy, Darci, and I found two half-empty paint cans and three corroded aluminum beach chairs in the garage. We dragged them out and sat on them along the edge of our driveway.

And waited.

Stella was arriving.

Mom and Ledward had gone to the airport to pick her up in Ledward's jeep.

"I've never seen a nanny before," Maya said.

"She's not a nanny! Jeese!"

"What is she, then?" Julio asked. "A babysitter?"

I leaned forward and put my head in my hands.

Maya bent close and whispered, "I bet she's pretty."

"Hey, Willy," Julio said. "Since she's a mainlander just like you, she won't even know what's a shave ice."

Willy humphed. "Or kimchee."

Julio laughed and slapped his knee. "Man, you should have seen the look on your face, ho, so funny!"

"How old is she?" Maya asked.

"Fifteen," Darci said. "Tenth grade."

Julio jumped up. "Here they come!"

My eyes were glued to Ledward's jeep as it came down the street. It was like a parade was coming, and we were waiting to see the queen.

Ledward honked as he pulled into the driveway.

Mom waved.

I gaped.

Stella from Texas was in the backseat. Wow, she was like a queen, all right. She glanced at us, brushing her long, windblown blond hair out of her eyes. A suitcase sat on one side of her, and a cardboard box on the other.

"She *is* pretty," Maya whispered.

Julio gawked. "Ho, man."

Stella just looked at us. Her eyes were light blue, and when she looked at me, I felt like she could see everything I ever in my life tried to hide.

I kept staring. I couldn't help it.

Ledward parked and turned off the engine.

"Is this the welcoming committee?" Mom asked.

I blinked and stumbled up. "Uh . . . yeah."

"That's so *nice*," Mom said. She got out and

hugged me. Over her shoulder, I saw Stella pull her hair back, revealing a glinting gold dot at the bottom of one ear.

"Thank you, Calvin. And thank all of *you,* too," Mom said to the rest of the welcoming committee.

Julio, Maya, and Willy gave Mom shy grins.

Darci was speechless, for once.

Stella stood up in the back of the jeep. She wore tight jeans and a blue shirt with white snap buttons. When Ledward reached up, she took his hand and stepped to the ground.

"These are my children," Mom said. "Calvin and Darci."

Darci asked, "Are you going to be my sister?"

Stella looked down at her. "Why would you think that, darlin'?"

Ho! She talks funny.

"And these three live in the neighbor-hood," Mom said. "Julio, Maya, and Willy."

Stella studied them.

Willy's mouth hung open, and I couldn't blame him. Stella's eyes were like magnets. You couldn't escape.

Willy looked down when Stella raised an eyebrow.

"Do you have a horse?" Maya asked. "I mean, in Texas?"

Stella turned to Maya, like, What kind of a stupid question is that? "No, I don't have a horse. But I have . . . I mean, I *had* . . . a para-keet. I guess it's my mom's now."

"What's a parakeet?" Julio asked.

"A small bird."

"Well," Mom said, clapping her hands once. "Want to see your new room, Stella?"

Stella shrugged.

Mom, Stella, and Darci headed into the house. Ledward grabbed the suitcase and box and fol-lowed them, making a face at me that said Yow!

Julio whistled low.

That night at dinner, Mom did all the talking. Darci watched Stella nibble. I shoveled my dinner down, keeping my eyes on my plate.

Mom reached over and put her hand on Stella's. "We are so happy to have you come live with us for a while." She glanced at me and Darci. "Aren't we, kids?"

"Yes!" Darci said, giving Stella her best smile.

Stella half smiled back, then glanced at me.

I held my fork in midair. "Uh, yeah. We're, uh, happy."

Stella's eyes narrowed, her half smile still plastered on.

I coughed and lowered my fork.

Stella turned to Mom. "They won't give me any trouble, will they?"

"These kids?" said Mom. "No trouble. No trouble at all."

That night, I lay on my back on the top bunk in my new room. In the corner just above my head, a small black spider slept in its web. "You like this room, spidey?"

The spider didn't move.

"That bad, huh?"

I turned over on my stomach and mashed my pillow up under my chin. The window was a black square of night. When I turned the light off, maybe I'd see the river.

Someone knocked and opened my door. "May I come in?"

"Sure, Mom."

"Wow," she said, looking around. "You and Ledward really got this place cleaned up. It looks great, don't you think?"

I rolled over and pointed to the spider. "See my new roommate?"

"Want me to get it for you?"

"No, he just sleeps."

Mom leaned against the counter that ran along one side of my new room. She crossed her arms and looked up at me. "There's a sweet girl under Stella's rough exterior, Calvin. I think she just needs to get to know us."

"She doesn't talk much."

"Give her time. She comes from a . . . well, a difficult situation. Her parents are struggling now. Her mom thought sending her here would help everyone, including me, and she's certainly right about that."

"Okay."

"You're old enough to take care of yourself now. But Darci needs someone at home while I'm at work."

"Stella could do the garbage," I offered. "That would free me up to cut the grass."

Mom laughed, a real, deep laugh. She pushed herself away from the counter and reached up to squeeze my hand. "I just don't know what I'd do without your good humor, Cal."

She kissed me good night and left.

I looked up at the spider. "What was so funny?"

# Oops

The next morning, Sunday, I was jolted out of my dreams.

"Calvin!"

I squinted at my clock. Eight-fifteen.

"Calvin! Get in here this *minute*!"

Mom didn't sound happy.

I slid off my bunk. I put on yesterday's

shorts and T-shirt and stumbled through the garage.

Mom stood in the kitchen with her arms crossed. "I told you to fix that lock on your door."

Oops. "I . . . forgot."

"Yes, you forgot, and now Stella is stuck in her room. What are you going to do about it?"

"Um, I can get it open."

"So get to it!"

I ran to my old bedroom and knocked on the door. "Uh . . . Stella?"

"Unlock this door!"

"It's just supposed to pop open when you turn the knob."

"Well, I'm turning and it's not popping. Your mom said you could get it open, so do it. I need to go to the bathroom."

I tried the knob.

Locked, all right. "Uh . . . try turning and lifting at the same time."

Stella huffed and grunted, then banged her fist on the door. "Get me out of here!"

"Wait. Be right back."

I ran to my room, grabbed my pocketknife, and ran back. "Look by your feet." I slid the knife under the door.

"What's this for?"

"Stick the blade in the slot on the thumb lock, then turn it. That's how I get it open."

I could hear her working the knife into the doorknob. "You better not be joking around with me."

"I'm not. Turn it like a key."

"I'm not kidding, buster, if you're—" She banged the door again. "It! Doesn't! Work!"

"Okay, wait! I'll be back."

"I've had enough of this, buster!"

I raced out to the garage. Boy, she was getting mean. Could I help it if the lock always got stuck?

"Did you get it open?" Mom asked as I ran through the kitchen.

"Not yet."

"Where are you going?"

"Hammer and a screwdriver."

"You're not going to break down the door, are you?"

"I'm going to take it off its hinges. Julio did that once."

I started toward the garage.

"Wait," Mom said. "The hinges are on the inside."

I hesitated. "They are?"

"Of course they are. What good is a lock if they're on the outside? Anyone could just do what you're planning to do."

"Oh." I slumped against the doorjamb. "Then I think she's going to have to climb out the window."

Mom put the palm of her hand to her forehead. "If you could just for once have shown a little responsibility and fixed that lock, we wouldn't be having this problem."

"Sorry."

Mom sighed. "Go tell her."

Darci called as I passed her room. She was sitting in her bed rubbing her eyes. "What's all the noise?"

"Stella's stuck in her room. She has to climb out the window."

Darci leaped out of bed. "I want to see!"

"Calvin!" Mom called from the kitchen.

"Yeah?"

"I have to leave now. I'm supposed to meet Ledward at Costco, and there's no way I can contact him. Get Stella out of that room, you understand?"

"Yeah, Mom. I'll get her out."

"I'll be home sometime this afternoon. You and Darci do everything Stella tells you. She's in charge while I'm gone, is that clear?"

Great.

"Yeah, it's clear."

The kitchen door banged shut. I heard the car start.

Then Julio showed up.

"Calvin," he called from the front door. He cupped his hands around his eyes and looked through the screen. "Come out."

I ran to the door. "Wait . . . I have to do something first."

"I'll be out back on Darci's swing," Julio said.

I crept up to Stella's door. "Stella?"

"What."

"Um . . . you have to, uh, to climb out the window."

Silence.

"Stella?"

"You did this on purpose, didn't you?"

"What? No!"

"You're going to pay for this."

"But I didn't—"

"What's your favorite color?"

"What?"

"Color, your favorite color."

"Blue?"

"I'll tell everyone to bring blue flowers, then."

"Bring them to what?"

"Your funeral. When I get out of here, you're dead."

# 18

# Holy Bazooks!

Darci followed me out the sliding patio door. The rusty chain squeaked as Julio slowly kicked back and forth over the muddy puddle beneath the swing. "Something going on?"

"Stella has to climb out the window," Darci said.

Julio looked at me. "Lock stuck again?"

Stella was at the window, scowling.

"Calvin was supposed to fix it."

"Hey, you!" somebody called. "Calvin Coco-dork."

Tito and Frankie Diamond had pulled themselves up on the back side of our fence. Their heads and hands were all I could see.

"Go in the house," I said to Darci. "Talk to Stella through the door."

"Why?"

"Just go."

Darci left, glancing back at Tito and Frankie Diamond.

Julio jumped off the swing.

"You and me still got business to settle," Tito said.

"Why?" I said, which was probably the dumbest thing I could ever have said at a time like that.

Tito scoffed. "You owe me a new shirt, that's why. . . . Oh, and I owe you a broken face."

Tito pulled himself higher, as if he was going to jump over into our yard.

But he stopped when Stella banged the screen off the window. I turned to look back. Stella poked her head out, then pulled herself up and hung out over the windowsill on her gut.

I whipped back around to see if Tito was coming over the fence to get me. No. He was gaping at Stella.

I turned to Stella just in time to see her tumble headfirst out the window in her hot-pink shortie pajamas. She flipped and fell flat on her butt in the muddy grass. *"Ooof!"*

I winced.

Stella staggered up and brushed herself off. Her face went bright red when she saw four boys staring at her.

No one peeped.

Stella glared rusty razors, mostly at me, then headed inside through the sliding patio door. I flinched when she slammed it shut.

"Holy bazooks," Tito said. "Who was *that*?"

I didn't answer. I was busy wondering: How mean could Stella get? And who's going to kill me first? Tito or Stella?

"Hey!" Tito snapped. "I asked you a question. Who was that? Your sister?"

"No, uh . . . she—"

"She just moved in with them," Julio said. "Her name is Stella."

Tito grinned. "Stel-la," he said, slow. "I like that name."

Frankie Diamond dropped out of sight behind the fence.

Tito said, "Ten minutes, Coco-dork. Then I

come your front yard and we can finish our business. And tell Stel-la come out . . . after I mess you up I might ask her for go beach. Least you could do for me, ah?"

Tito let go and vanished.

Julio shook his head. "Hoo, glad I'm not you."

"I'm dead."

"Yeah, and you're dead again when you go in the house. Either way, you're history."

I paced. "You think the army takes nine-year-olds?"

"No, but the undertaker does." Julio laughed.

While Julio was enjoying his own bad joke, I ran to Stella's window and dropped over the sill into my old room. My pocketknife was on the floor by the door. I grabbed it and worked the blade into the slot on the knob. The lock popped. Jeese. That was easy. I opened the door and ran back to the window before I got caught in there.

Stella burst out the patio door seconds after

I tumbled from the window. She had a towel around her waist now and was looking for revenge.

Me and Julio took off to the front yard like spooked mice.

# 19

## wax

We found Willy pounding on the front door. "Hide," he gasped. "Look who's coming!"

Tito and Frankie Diamond were swaggering down the street. My scalp tingled with fear. "The fort!"

We ran into the jungle across the street.

In the summer Julio and I had dug a pit in

the sand. We'd covered it with boards and jungle trash, so it looked like a pile of rubbish. Inside, a cardboard box made a table, with a candle for light. Hiding in the fort was as good as being invisible.

I lifted a corner of the trash pile. We slipped in and disappeared.

Julio fumbled around in the dark for the matches. He lit the candle. Light wobbled on his face.

"Wow," Willy said. "This is nice!"

"Sinbad will never find us in here."

I cocked my ear, listening. I put a finger over my lips. Nobody moved. We sat, silent.

Above, voices mumbled in the jungle.

Thin rays of light streaked through the cracks.

"They're close," Tito said.

He was nearly on top of us. I blew out the candle.

"I think they went out on the golf course," Frankie Diamond said.

I heard the crunching of dry leaves and

jungle trash as Tito and Frankie Diamond moved around overhead. I imagined them hunched over, like soldiers on patrol.

The crunching stopped.

I held my breath.

"You smell wax?" Frankie Diamond said.

"Wax?"

"Like a candle."

I squeezed my eyes shut. Why did I blow it out? Dumb, dumb, dumb.

"I don't smell no wax," Tito said.

"I do," Frankie Diamond said.

I looked up through the peepholes in the boards and thought I could see a piece of Tito's back.

"They gone," Tito said. "We go."

"Fine, but I'm telling you, I smell . . ."

Their voices faded away.

I let out my breath. I wanted to say, Man, that was *close*! But I was way too scared.

"Ho," Julio finally said. "My heart is pounding."

"What would he do if he caught you?" Willy asked.

"You ever see a cat eat a bird?" I said.

"Yeah."

"Like that."

Julio elbowed me. "Let's go on your boat. You're safe on the river, unless Tito swims after you . . . if he knows how."

"Yeah," I said, seeing a small glint of hope. "He can't get us there."

"Not us," Julio said. "You."

I poked my head out of the sand pit. The coast was clear. We crawled out. Willy and Julio followed me through the jungle.

I kept my red skiff in the long swamp grass at the bottom of our yard. Two oars were tucked under the middle seat.

We dragged the skiff to the water. It wobbled as Willy and Julio climbed in. I pushed off and jumped aboard after them.

Willy sat in the bow. Julio settled into the stern seat. I sat in the middle and rowed upriver, not down toward the ocean, where Tito could trap us like mullet in the shallow waters near the beach.

Willy's face lit up. "Look at this place," he whispered.

Along the shore, a thick mangrove jungle bulged out over the water. Dark, glassy coves sat back in mysterious inlets. If there were snakes in Hawaii, they'd be hanging like vines from the branches.

Just upriver, a rickety wooden bridge crossed from one side of the river to the other. Golfers pulled their carts over it. Willy looked up at the creaky wood slats as I rowed under it. "This is so awesome!"

"Didn't you have rivers in California?" Julio asked.

"Sure, but not like–"

Julio turned when something plunked in

the water just
behind him.
"Jeez, those
guys follow us
around like germs."

Tito and Frankie Diamond were down by
the water in my yard. Tito threw another rock.
This time it almost reached the bridge.

I rowed upstream. Fast.

Tito couldn't throw that far.

I let the skiff drift, rowing just enough to
keep from moving back downriver.

Tito and Frankie Diamond walked up the
slope of my yard and sat on the grass.

"They're going to wait," Julio said.

I felt sick.

Willy said, "At my old school in Pasadena, if you let somebody push you around,
they'd just keep doing it. But if you stood up
to them . . . sometimes they stopped bother-
ing you."

"Sometimes?"

"My dad said guys like that are cowards.

And cowards go after cowards, not guys who stand up to them."

I stared at Willy.

Willy shrugged. "That's what he said."

"Willy's right," Julio said. "You can't just sit out here forever. Sooner or later you got to . . . you know . . . do something."

I didn't like where this conversation was going. "What am I supposed to do? Just let him beat me up?"

"No," Willy said. "You face him down."

"How?"

Willy squinted across the water at Tito, who was on the grass, leaning back on his elbows. "You'll think of something."

# 20

# Really Good Friends

Tito stood when the skiff slid into the swamp grass at the bottom of my yard. He was still wearing his ruined *SmackDown* T-shirt. Frankie Diamond leaned back on his hands to watch the show.

We stepped out of the skiff and dragged it farther up into the swamp grass. I stowed the oars under the seat. Take your time.

*And think of something!*

Tito strolled down to me. "You should know by now that you can't run away from Tito."

I had to force myself not to jump into the skiff and push it back out into the water.

Julio and Willy retreated when Tito glanced at them.

Up the slope, Frankie Diamond grinned.

*Think!*

But my mind was blank.

Tito looked down at his shirt. "Look at this. Junk, now. I got to throw it away."

"It was an accident."

Tito slammed my chest with the palms of his hands.

I staggered back.

"Oh. Sorry," Tito said. "That was an accident."

*Think of something! Now!*

Tito stepped up to slam me again.

I put up my hand. "Wait! I'll buy you a new shirt."

Tito laughed. "How? My uncle got me it at

*SmackDown.* They gone now, so how you going buy me one new one?"

"I'll . . . I'll give you something, then."

"What you got I want? LEGOs?"

Behind him Frankie Diamond stuffed a
laugh. Tito turned and grinned at him.

The screen door slapped open, and Tito
glanced toward the house. When he saw
Stella, his grin turned into a crooked smile.

Stella crossed her arms. Darci stood next to
her, both of them watching.

Tito turned back to me. "Like I was saying, Coco-loser . . . what you got I want?"

"I have . . . I have . . ."

"I give you one minute to think of something good," Tito said. "I'm a generous person."

*Tick . . . tick . . . tick.*

I thought.

And for once in my life an idea came roaring up. That's it! "I'll introduce you to . . . her." I lifted my chin toward Stella.

Tito looked over his shoulder.

Stella squinted, too far away to hear us.

"We're really good friends," I went on. "She just came to live with us. She has a . . . a horse."

Stella glared at me. She knew I was talking about her.

"Now you talking like a man, Coco-bug," Tito said.

"Her name is—"

"Stel-la," Tito said dreamily. "What grade she's in?"

"Tenth."

"I like older women."

Julio laughed, but quickly pretended to be coughing when Tito looked his way. Then back at me. "You got a deal, Coco-punk. You introduce me to Stella, I let you live."

Relief rolled off my back. "She's really friendly, Tito, you'll like her."

Tito clapped me on the back like we were good friends. Frankie Diamond threw his head back and laughed. Tito waggled his eyebrows at him.

We headed up the slope.

Stella looked friendly . . . as a shark. Maybe she always looked angry.

"Uh, Stella," I said, not getting too close. "Um . . . this is . . . my friend, Tito. Tito, this is Stella. . . . She's from Texas."

Tito seemed to have lost his words. He stood smiling that crooked smile at Stella, but the smile was frozen.

"Your friend, huh?" Stella said.

"Yeah . . . from school."

"I saw him push you," Stella said.

I fake-laughed. "Oh, that . . . we were just fooling around. Right, Tito?"

Tito stared, still frozen.

"What's up with your shirt?" she asked.

I elbowed Tito.

Tito blinked. "Uh . . . what?"

"Your shirt," Stella said. "You always wear rags?"

"Oh, this? I always wear my junk ones when I go . . . uh, hunting."

Stella looked at Tito, like, Are you an idiot?

"Yeah," Tito said. "Me and Frankie . . ." He turned and waved a hand in Frankie's direction. "We was going my uncle's house today . . . to go pig hunting, you know, in the mountains."

Stella looked at Tito a moment longer, then

put her hand on Darci's shoulder and headed back toward the house. When the screen door slapped shut behind them, Tito said, "She likes me."

"Oh, yeah, Tito," I said. "You the man, hunting pigs, hoo, girls like guys who do that kind of stuff."

"Man style, ah?"

"Man style, you got it."

Tito gazed back at my house. "You think she likes dried shrimp?"

"Sure," I said. "Who doesn't like dried shrimp?"

# 21

# Texas Nice

Ledward and Mom came home when the sun was low and the sky was pink. I went out and helped Ledward unload all the stuff they got at Costco.

"You want to stay for dinner, Led?" Mom asked.

"Sure do, but I gotta get home, feed my dogs."

Mom nodded. "Well, thanks for all your help, and thanks for helping Calvin clean out the storeroom."

"No problem." Ledward put his huge hand on my shoulder. "How's that room working out?"

"Fine."

"And the girl? You like her?"

I shrugged.

Ledward chuckled. "Hard to be the only boy with all these girls. You should get a dog."

Yeah. A dog.

That night, Mom made meat loaf, string beans, and sweet potatoes. I sat at the head of the table, where the man of the house was supposed to sit.

"Cal," Mom said. "Why don't you let Stella sit there."

I looked up. What?

"She's our guest."

I frowned and moved across from Darci, and though I wanted to complain, I didn't.

Stella had sort of saved my life that day. I owed her.

Stella sat in my place at the head of the table. She said nothing.

"So, Cal," Mom said. "How do you like school? You haven't told me anything."

"It's good. I like Mr. Purdy."

"Good, I'm glad. And how about you, Stella?" Mom went on. "Do you like the islands so far?"

"Ain't got no complaints," she said. "I like the beach."

"*Ain't* isn't a word," I said. I'd learned that in school.

Stella winked at me. "It is where I come from, honey."

Mom turned to Darci. "Did you and Calvin have any problems walking home on Friday? I forgot to ask."

Busted!

"He talked to my teacher," Darci said. "She's nice."

Thank you, thank you, thank you! I'll

never forget you again in my whole life, Darce, I promise.

"And everything went well?" Mom asked.

"Yep."

I felt lighter. I even smiled at Stella.

"Thank you, Calvin," Mom said. "It really helps to know that I can count on you to be responsible."

I grunted, and stuffed my mouth with meat loaf.

Someone rapped on the screen door.

"Go see who that is, Cal," Mom said.

I got up and turned the porch light on. On the other side of the screen door, Tito smiled.

My stomach sank. I pushed open the door.

"Heyyy, Coco-my-man," Tito said like a nice person. "I brought Stella something. Give her it for me, ah? Tell her it's a present . . . from Tito."

I blinked as Tito handed me a brand-new bag of dried shrimp. Who did he steal it from at this late hour?

"Don't you want to give it to her yourself?"

"No—no," Tito said. "I gotta go." In a flash he was gone.

"Close the door!" Mom called. "You're letting the mosquitoes in."

I stood holding the dried shrimp and watching Tito hurry off. Ho, I thought. What have I started?

"Who was it?" Mom asked, back at the table.

I held up the bag of dried shrimp. "Tito brought this over for Stella. It's a present."

"Ho, how nice, Stella," Mom said. "You're already making new friends."

Stella snapped the bag from my hand. "What is this?" She looked closely, and when she saw the tiny, shriveled-up, orangy-red shrimps, with their legs curled and no heads, she shrieked and tossed the bag back at me.

"That's disgusting!" she spat. "That dumb kid brought me a bag of bugs?"

"No," I said. "It's dried shrimp. They're good."

"For what? Fertilizer?"

"Here, try some." I tore the bag open.

"Calvin," Mom said. "Stella needs time to get used to the foods we eat here. Put the shrimp away."

"*Throw* it away, you mean," Stella said.

"Stella." Mom put a hand on her arm.

"Can I have it?" I asked.

"*You* did this," Stella said, glaring at me with those light blue eyes. "What did you tell him, anyway? Why did he bring that . . . that revolting bag of dried-up bugs to me?"

"They're not bugs!" I shouted.

"Put the shrimp away in the kitchen, Calvin," Mom said. "Then come back and finish your dinner."

"I'm just saying, they're not bugs."

Stella squinted. "What does it mean around here when someone brings you a bag of bugs? Is it some kind of insult or something?"

"No," I said. "He's just being nice."

"*Nice?* He does that again, I'll show him nice. Texas nice. Maybe I'll show you some Texas nice, too, for getting me into this mess."

I hurried into the kitchen. Whatever Texas nice was, I didn't want to know.

# 22

# who Doesn't Like Calvin Coconut?

Later that night, I was in my room craving vanilla ice cream with chocolate syrup oozing down all over it. And crushed Oreos. My mouth watered just thinking about it.

But Mom never bought that stuff. "Have a banana," she always said when I was hungry. "Put peanut butter on it."

I settled for Stella's dried shrimp.

They were chewy, salty, and delicious. They also made me thirsty, so I slipped off my bunk and went into the house for a drink of water.

Darci must have been starving, too, because I caught her in the kitchen with her hand deep into a box of Frosted Mini-Wheats. "Want some?" she said, eating them right out of the box.

"Where's Mom?"

Darci took the cereal box and peeked around the corner. "Asleep on the couch."

Sure enough, Mom was slumped over with her feet up on the coffee table. Her reading glasses were halfway down her nose, and her book was closed over her finger.

"Hey, twerp," someone said.

I hadn't noticed Stella. She was lounging on the floor, reading a magazine. The TV was on with the sound off. Without looking up, she said, "Isn't it past your bedtime?"

I retreated into the kitchen. "Didn't take long for her to get bossy, did it?"

"It's your bedtime, too, Darci," Stella called.

"What?" Mom said groggily. "Did you say something, Stella? I must have fallen asleep."

"I was just telling your children it's their bedtime . . . school night, you know."

"Right, school night." Mom yawned again. "Calvin? Are you and Darci in the kitchen?"

I rolled my eyes at Darci.

Darci giggled.

"Yeah . . . I was just getting a snack."

"Have a banana, and then you and Darci brush your teeth and get ready for bed, okay?"

"Sure, Mom."

Darci grabbed one last handful of cereal and stuffed it into her pocket.

"Look," I said, pulling the bag of dried shrimp out of my pocket. "Dead bugs."

Darci laughed.

"What are you laughing at in there?" Stella called.

Man, she has ears like a dog. I poked my head out the door. "Nothing."

"No, I heard you say something to Darci. Are you laughing at me?"

I looked at Darci. "Did I say something funny, Darci?"

Darci grinned and shook her head.

"See?"

Stella squinted. "You'd better watch yourself, buster."

I grabbed Darci's hand. "Come on, Darce. Let's go find a mirror. I have to watch myself."

"Funny," Stella said.

"Just go brush your teeth, Calvin," Mom said.

In the bathroom I opened the first drawer, where Darci and I kept our toothbrushes. But it wasn't our drawer anymore. It was stuffed with Stella's junk. "She sure moved in fast."

Our stuff was now in the second drawer. I grabbed the gnarled, uncapped tube of toothpaste and scraped the

dried gunk away from the open-
ing with my thumbnail.

"I don't think Stella likes you,"
Darci said.

I squeezed toothpaste onto my
toothbrush, then Darci's. "She
likes me."

"It doesn't seem like she does."

"Who doesn't like Calvin
Coconut?"

Darci stopped brushing and
garbled, "Thah boy who waff
fighting wiff you?"

"We weren't fighting."

Darci turned on the water and
spat. "He pushed you."

"Yeah . . . but we're friends now."

I waited for Darci to finish with
the sink. Stella's stuff was all over
the place—bottles, tubes, rubber
bands, lotions, brushes, hair
dryer. She sure had a lot of junk.

"Darci?"

"Huh."

"Thanks for not telling Mom I messed up on Friday . . . you know, by forgetting to walk you home and all."

"That's okay."

"Do you feel bad about lying to her?"

"I didn't lie."

I thought back, trying to remember. Maybe she hadn't. Maybe she'd just changed the subject. I pulled a crumpled piece of paper out of my pocket. "Here, you want this?"

Darci took the paper and flattened it out.

I tapped it with my finger. "You can get a free shave ice at Uncle Scoop's Lucky Lunch with that."

"Really?"

"See it says *complimentary*? That means free. This paper is like money. You can have it."

"Thanks!" Darci said. She folded the coupon neatly and headed down the hall to her bedroom. She stopped and turned back. "Calvin?"

"Yeah."

"You can forget me again tomorrow . . . if you want to."

I smiled. "Nope. I'll be there. I'm pretty sure I don't need any more trouble. But thanks."

"Sure."

"Hey," I said, holding out the bag of dried shrimp. "Want some dead bugs to go with your cereal?"

Darci cracked up.

"Hey!" Stella called from the living room. "You want that Texas nice right now?"

Darci and I slapped our hands over our mouths, our eyes tearing with muffled laughter.

# 23

# Responsible

As I headed out to the garage, another idea came to me. "I need a screwdriver," I said to myself. I found one and went back into the house.

"I thought you were going to bed," Mom said.

"Got to do something first."

I went down the hall to Stella's bedroom door and unscrewed the plate around the doorknob. Next I worked the entire lockset off the door. It left a round hole you could look through into Stella's room. Boy, I hope Ledward knows something about locks, because I sure don't.

Stella looked up when I walked back out into the living room.

"You won't have a doorknob for a while. But I'm going to fix it for you."

Back in my room on my bunk, I turned off the light and settled onto my stomach. I tucked my pillow under my chin and looked out the window. I could see yellowy pieces of moon jiggling on the slow-moving river. The quirky cricking of toads in the swamp grass drifted through the screen.

Someone knocked on my door.

I popped up. "Yeah?"

"Can I come in?"

Stella.

"Uh . . . yeah."

She opened the door. "Can I turn the light on?"

"Okay."

Stella flipped the switch. "Your mom said this used to be a storage room."

"It was full of bugs and spiderwebs."

Stella leaned in but didn't actually enter. "Well . . . I just wanted to say thank you for letting me have your room."

"Uh . . . sure."

"But listen, you have to get that kid off my back. I don't want little tough guys bringing me any more bags of dried-up bugs, you understand?"

"Uh . . ."

"Good night."

Stella turned off the light and closed the door. I could hear her stumbling through the cluttered garage to the kitchen door.

I went back to looking out the window. How was I going to tell Tito that his Stella dream wasn't going to happen? I cringed. But I'd come up with something. I'd done it once; I could do it again. Right?

Someone knocked again.

The door opened, but the light stayed off. "Calvin? Still awake?"

"Yeah, Mom."

"I love you . . . lots. Good night."

Somewhere a dog barked.

I fell asleep quickly.

## A Hawaii Fact

Sometimes when you water your yard with a hose, centipedes come out of cracks in the earth and crawl up your pants.

## A Calvin Fact

After cleaning your ears, be sure creatures such as mice, lizards, roaches, and ants don't eat your earwax. That would make you deaf.